The Muppet Babies live in a nursery
in a house on a street that is a lot like yours.
But they can travel anywhere anytime using a special power—
the power of the imagination.
Can you imagine what it would be like to go with them?
Join the Muppet Babies on this adventure and find out.

Weekly Reader Presents

Kermit the Hermit

By Barry Keating • Illustrated by Tom Cooke

Muppet Press/Marvel

Weekly Reader Books offers several exciting
card and activity programs. For information,
write to WEEKLY READER BOOKS, P.O. Box 16636,
Columbus, Ohio 43216.

This book is a presentation of
Weekly Reader Books.

Weekly Reader Books offers book clubs for children
from preschool through high school.

For further information write to:
Weekly Reader Books
4343 Equity Drive
Columbus, Ohio 43228

ISBN 0-87135-095-5

It was spring-cleaning time in the nursery room,
And nothing was safe from the dust mop and broom.
Nanny had hired a house-cleaning crew
To make the whole nursery shiny and new.

They shampooed the furniture, dusted the toys,
And filled the whole room with confusion and noise.
Kermit had nowhere to read or to play.
He wished that the strangers would just go away.

"Too many people!" thought poor little Kermit.
"Life would be better if I were a hermit!"

A hermit is someone who lives all alone
In a cave with no furniture, TV, or phone.

There's nobody there, so it's peaceful and quiet—
"That's just what I want," figured Kermit. "I'll try it."

So he scrunched up his eyes and let his thoughts wander
To an empty old cave in the hills way up yonder,
An echoing cavern with no one in sight.
"Now I'll be a hermit!" he said with delight.

He got a big stick, and he grew a long beard,
For hermits, thought Kermit, should look a bit weird.

He crawled through the cave—every crook, nook, and cranny.
There was nobody there—no house-cleaners, no Nanny,
No one to talk to, no friends big or small,
No playmates to play with, no people at all.
It was *too* calm and quiet. There was nothing to do.
He needed excitement—a stranger or two!

Skrinch! came a sound which startled poor Kermit,
And up through the floor popped a worm named McDermott.

"I bring you good news," said the worm. "Pay attention—
Your cave is the site of a hermit convention.
And you shall be chairman of all the great hermits,
And give out the prizes and hermitting permits."

"I'll do it!" said Kermit politely but proudly.
Just then someone knocked on the door rather loudly.

"Is this Kermit's cave?" called an old hermit crab.
Then he sat on a boulder and started to gab.

He talked about hermits that some folks call Lamas,
Who shave off their hair and wear burlap pajamas.
Just as he mentioned them, several walked in,
Singing and making a glorious din!

The crab then told Kermit of hermits called Monks,
Who sleep on the mountain in creaky old bunks,
And live on a diet of sausage and ham,
And paste little labels on bottles of jam.

Just as Old Crabby had mentioned their name,
Into that cavern the merry Monks came,
Carrying poles (for they do love to shinny 'em),
Converting the cave to a Monk condominium.

New hermits walked in—they were young ones called Rookies,
Munching and lunching on fresh hermit cookies.

Beachcombing hermits brought barrels of sand.
Hermits with horns formed an all hermit band.

Hermits kept coming—more hermits—then more!
They could hardly all fit through that little cave door.
Hermits with pets and hermits in pairs,
Small hermit turtles and big hermit bears.

Hermits with feathers and hermits who sneezed,
Hairy old hermits who did as they pleased.
Fat ones and skinny ones, all shapes and sizes,
Danced up to Kermit for permits and prizes.

The cave was so full, Kermit had to cry, "Stop!"
And just as he did, his dream broke with a pop!

The cave disappeared. He was back in his room
With Nanny, the cleaners, the dust mop, and broom.

But now that his hermit adventure was done,
He knew that a big noisy crowd could be fun.
So he grabbed up a broom and helped out like a friend.
"I'm proud of you, Kermit," said Nanny...

...THE END.